Edition 1
The Hungry Hamster who ate the moon!
AniMEALs

Author - Jacob Fretwell
Illustrations - Jacob Fretwell & Lauren Clithero
Digital art - Lauren Clithero

Printed in the United Kingdom

First Printing, 2019

ISBN 9781696940528

Independently published
Kindle Direct Publishing
Amazon, UK

www.amazon.co.uk

THE HUNGRY HAMSTER WHO ATE THE MOON,
STARTED OFF BY EATING A spoon.

teaspoon

EVER SO HUNGRY HE STARTED TO CRY.

TO CHEER HIMSELF UP,

LOVING THE PIE HE MADE FIVE MORE,

HE SWALLOWED ONE WHOLE,

FOLLOWED BY FOUR!

THIS HUNGRY HAMSTER IS GETTING QUITE **FAT**,

He ate the cat and munched on a horse,

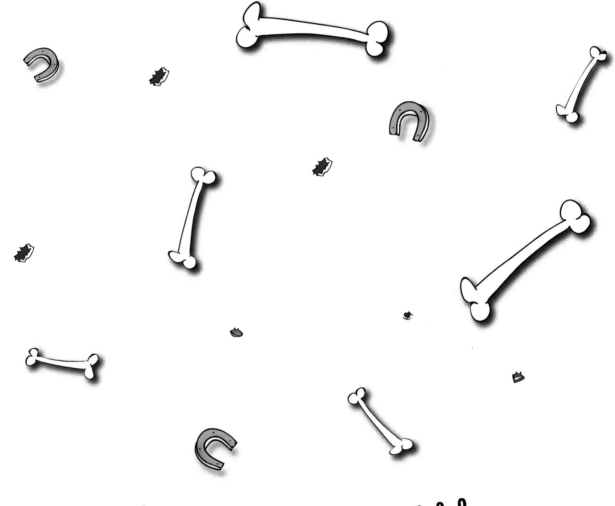

Is he still hungry???

HE MIGHT EAT ME!

HE GOBBLED ME UP   AND   SPAT ME BACK OUT,

HE'S TOO FULL,

OH NO!

WATCH OUT!

HE'S TAKEN OFF AND GOING TO THE MOON,

HEY LOOK!

THERE'S THAT
SPOON!

LANDING SAFELY ON HIS FEET,

THE MOON LOOKS TASTY,

IT'S READY TO EAT!

TWO YEARS LATER,

ONLY HALF WAY THROUGH,

OH GOLLY GOSH,

THE HUNGRY HAMSTER

QUIZ

1. How many pies did the hungry hamster eat?

....

2. What did the hungry hamster eat first?

————————————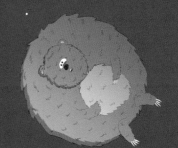

3. What colour is the cat that the hungry hamster eats?

....

4. Can you name three other kinds of rodents?

....

5. How long does it take the hungry hamster to eat half of the moon?

....

Draw THE HUNGRY HAMSTER

EATING YOUR FAVOURITE FOOD!

Name & draw **YOUR OWN** hamster!

NAME:

WHAT WOULD HE BE EATING?

FUN FACTS

about hamsters!

1. Hamsters are more active at night.

2. There are over 25 species of hamsters around the world - from LARGE ones to tiny dwarfs ones!

3. The LARGEST breed of hamster is European, called 'Cricetus Cricetus' - that can mesure up to 34cm / 13.4inches long!

4. tiny DWARF hamsters are the smallest breeds, called 'genus Phodopus' - mesuring as small as 5.08cm / 2 inches!

5. Male hamsters are called 'boars'.

6. Female hamsters are called 'sows'.

7. Baby hamsters are called 'pups'.

8. Hamsters are omnivores - meaning they like to eat meat & vegetables!

9. Hamsters like to store food in their cheeks, to eat later.

10. Hamsters are colour blind!

Cut Out THE HUNGRY HAMSTER

& MAKE A COLLAGE ON THE NEXT PAGE!

REMEMBER TO GET AN ADULT TO HELP YOU!

Printed in Poland
by Amazon Fulfillment
Poland Sp. z o.o., Wrocław